E
MO

Moncure, Jane Belk

Word Bird makes
words with Pig

DATE			
AG 17 '85	MY 8 '86	AG 17 '8	MR 6 '90
Aug. 20 1985	MY 17 '86	JY 14 '88	AG 20 '90
SE 11 '85		DE 15 '88	SE 27 '90
OCT. 21 1985	JE 06 '86	JA 28 '89	
OC 31 '85	JE 21 '86	FE 29 '89	MR 8 '91
NO 23 '85	JY 7 '86	MY 15 '89	AG 22 '91
DE 13 '85	AG 19 '86		DE 10 '91
JA 24 '86	JA 26 '87	JY 5 '89	JY 8 '92
FE 25 '86	AP 10 '87	JY 24 '89	JY 20 '92
AP 1 '86	MY 28 '87	AG 10 '89	AG 13 '92
	JY 6 '87	AG 22 '89	JL 7 '93
		FE 17 '90	JAN 27 '96
			AUG 31 '98
			JUN 05 '99

EAU CLAIRE DISTRICT LiBRARY

WORD BIRD
MAKES WORDS WITH PIG

by Jane Belk Moncure
illustrated by Vera Gohman

THE
CHILD'S
WORLD

ELGIN, ILLINOIS 60120

We acknowledge with gratitude the review of the Word Bird Short Vowel Adventure *books by Dr. John Mize, Director of Reading, Alamance County Schools, Graham, North Carolina.*

—The Child's World

Distributed by Childrens Press, 1224 West Van Buren Street, Chicago, Illinois 60607.

Library of Congress Cataloging in Publication Data

Moncure, Jane Belk.
  Word Bird makes words with Pig.
  — A short "i" adventure.

  (Word Bird's short vowel adventures)
  Summary: Word Bird makes up more words with his friend Pig. Each word that they make up leads them into a new activity.
  [1. Vocabulary. 2. Birds—Fiction. 3. Pigs—Fiction] I. Gohman, Vera Kennedy, 1922- , ill.
II. Title. III. Series: Moncure, Jane Belk. Word Bird's short vowel adventures.
PZ7.M739Wnp 1984   [E]   83-23945
ISBN 0-89565-262-5

2 3 4 5 6 7 8 9 10 11 12 R 91 90 89 88 87 86 85 84

WORD BIRD

MAKES WORDS WITH PIG

"Did you bring some word puzzles?" asked Word Bird.

"I did," said Papa.

"I can make words in
a jiffy," said Word Bird.

He put

What word did Word Bird make?

Just then his friend, Pig, came to play.

"Hi, Pig."

"I can make words too," said Pig.

She put  w with ig

What word did Pig make?

wig

"I like wigs," said Pig.
"Do you want to see
my wigs?"

Pig put a wig on Word
Bird. "What a silly wig!"
he said.

Pig giggled.

Then Pig made another word. She put

r with ing

What word did Pig make?

"Let's play dress up,"
she said. "I will wear
a wig and lots of rings."

"I will dress up too," said Word Bird.

He put

k with ing

What word did Word Bird make?

king

Word Bird played that he was king until Pig began to sing.

Then Word Bird made
another word in a jiffy.

He put

sw with ing

What word did he
make?

swing

"Let's go play on the swing," said Pig.

Word Bird gave Pig a big push in the swing.

Pig gave Word Bird a
big push in the swing.

"I will make another word," said Pig. She put

d with ish

What word did she make?

dish

"You need something in your dish," said Word Bird.

Just then Mama said, "Come to dinner."

Pig filled her dish
with figs.

After dinner, Pig helped
Word Bird wash all the
dishes.

"Now, what can we do?" asked Pig.

"I will make another word," said Word Bird. He put

sh with ip

What word did he make?

ship

"I have a ship," said Word Bird. "Let's take a trip in my ship."

And they did.

"I know something else we can do," said Pig. She put

f with ish

What word did Pig make?

f ish

24

"I will go fishing," she said.

Pig caught a big, big fish...

but the fish slipped away!

So Word Bird said, "Let's get off this ship and go home in a jiffy."

"Let's race!" said Pig.
"I will win."

"No," said Word Bird.
"I will win."

Suddenly, Word Bird
tripped and slipped.

Pig said, "I win." And she danced a jig all the way home.

You can read more word puzzles with

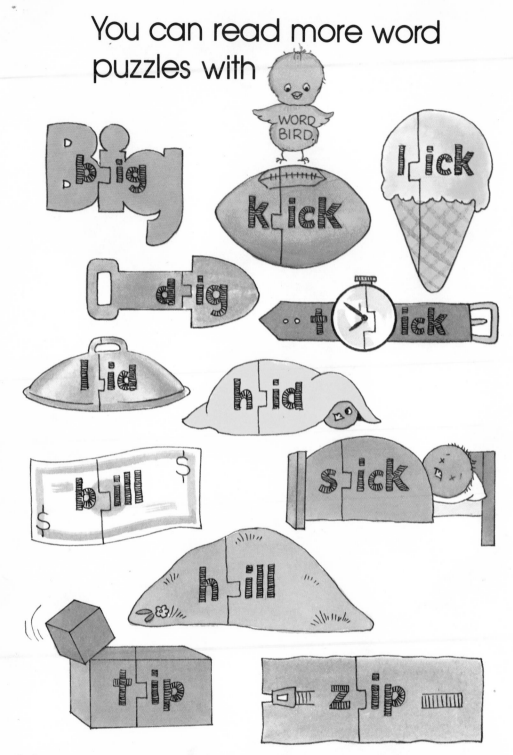

WORD BIRD.

Bbig

kick

l lick

dig

t ick

lid

hid

bill

sick

hill

tip

zip

Now you make more word puzzles.